Ecclesiastes

to everything there is a season

cynthia rylant

BEACH LANE BOOKS

New York   London   Toronto   Sydney   New Delhi

To everything there is a season
and a time to every purpose
under the heaven:

A time to be born,

and a time to die.

A time to plant,

and a time to pluck up that
which has been planted.

A time to break down,

and a time to build up.

A time to weep,

and a time to laugh.

A time to keep,

and a time to cast away.

A time of war,

and a time of peace.

God has made everything beautiful in his time.

And the earth abides forever.

BEACH LANE BOOKS

An imprint of Simon & Schuster Children's Publishing Division

1230 Avenue of the Americas, New York, New York 10020

Copyright © 2018 by Cynthia Rylant

The text for this book was adapted from chapter three of the Book of Ecclesiastes from the King James Version of the Holy Bible.

All rights reserved, including the right of reproduction in whole or in part in any form.

BEACH LANE BOOKS is a trademark of Simon & Schuster, Inc.

For information about special discounts for bulk purchases, please contact Simon & Schuster Special Sales

at 1-866-506-1949 or business@simonandschuster.com.

The Simon & Schuster Speakers Bureau can bring authors to your live event. For more information or to book an event,

contact the Simon & Schuster Speakers Bureau at 1-866-248-3049 or visit our website at www.simonspeakers.com.

For JD

Book design by Ann Bobco

The text for this book was set in Grit Primer.

The illustrations for this book were rendered in acrylic paints on Strathmore 140-lb. cold press watercolor paper.

Manufactured in China

0718 SCP

First Edition

2 4 6 8 10 9 7 5 3 1

Library of Congress Cataloging-in-Publication Data

Names: Rylant, Cynthia, illustrator.

Title: Ecclesiastes : to everything there is a season / Cynthia Rylant.

Other titles: Bible. Ecclesiastes, III, 1–11. English. Authorized. 2018.

Description: First edition. || New York : Beach Lane Books, 2018. || Includes bibliographical references and index.

Audience: Ages 0–8. || Audience: K to Grade 3.

Identifi ers: LCCN 2017061329 || ISBN 9781481476546 (hardcover : alk. paper) || ISBN 9781481476553 (eBook)

Subjects: LCSH: Bible. Ecclesiastes, III, 1–11—Illustrations.

Classifi cation: LCC BS1473.A88 2018 || DDC 223/.8052034—dc23 LC record available at https://lccn.loc.gov/2017061329